Parenting an Infant

by Kristin Thoennes Keller

Consultant:
Angela Thompson-Busch, MD, PhD
President/CEO
All About Children Pediatrics, PA
Eden Prairie, Minnesota

SKILLS FOR TEENS WHO PARENT

LifeMatters
an imprint of Capstone Press
Mankato, Minnesota

LifeMatters Books are published by Capstone Press
PO Box 669 • 151 Good Counsel Drive • Mankato, Minnesota 56002
http://www.capstone-press.com

©2001 Capstone Press. All rights reserved. No part of this book may be reproduced or transmitted in any form or by any means without written permission from the publisher.

SPECIAL ADVISORY: The information within this book concerns sensitive and important issues about which parental and teen discretion is advised. Because this book is general in nature, the reader should consult an appropriate health, medical, or other professional for advice. The publisher and its consultants take no responsibility for the use of any of the materials or methods described in this book nor for the products thereof.

Printed in the United States of America

Library of Congress Cataloging-in-Publication Data
Thoennes Keller, Kristin.
    Parenting an infant / by Kristin Thoennes Keller.
        p.   cm.—(Skills for teens who parent)
    Includes bibliographical references and index.
    Summary: Provides information on infant development and advice on how to care for a child for the first twelve months of its life, including facts about feeding, sleeping, crying, and other concerns.
    ISBN 0-7368-0702-0 (book)
    1. Teenage parents—Juvenile literature. 2. Child rearing—Juvenile literature. 3. Infants—Juvenile literature [1. Teenage parents. 2. Child rearing. 3. Infants.] I. Title. II. Series.
    HQ759.64 .T46 2001
    649´122—dc21   00-035226
                                                                            CIP

Staff Credits
Rebecca Aldridge, editor; Adam Lazar, designer; Kim Danger, photo researcher

Photo Credits
Cover: Stock Market/©Ariel Skelley, large; ©Digital Vision, top; ©Stockbyte, middle; PhotoDisc/©Barbara Penoyar, bottom
International Stock/©Laurie Bayer, 37
©Kimberly Danger, 32
Photo Network/©Myrleen Ferguson Cate, 22; ©Eric R. Berndt, 27; ©Esbin-Anderson, 28
©Stockbyte, 47
Unicorn Stock Photos/©A. Ramey, 14; ©Ann Woelfle Bater, 25; ©Eric R. Berndt, 41, 54; ©Martha McBride, 42; ©Steve Bourgeois, 50
Uniphoto/7, ©Llewellyn, 17, 57; ©Jeffry Myers, 48
Visuals Unlimited/©N. P. Alexander, 9; ©S. Folz, 19; ©D. Yeske, 59

A 0 9 8 7 6 5 4 3 2 1

Table of Contents

1	The First Month	4
2	Health and Safety for Your New Baby	12
3	Breastfeeding and Bottlefeeding	20
4	Introducing Solids	30
5	Your Baby: 1 to 3 Months	38
6	Your Baby: 4 to 7 Months	44
7	Your Baby: 8 to 12 Months	52
	For More Information	60
	Glossary	62
	Index	63

Chapter Overview

- Holding a new baby as often as possible is important to the relationship between parent and child.

- Babies cry often and for many reasons. There are ways to help calm your crying baby.

- Babies always should be placed on their back for sleeping.

- Frequently changing diapers can help prevent diaper rash.

- Give your baby sponge baths until the umbilical cord falls off. After that, use only a couple inches or a few centimeters of water for bathing. Never leave your baby alone in the bathtub.

CHAPTER 1

The First Month

Introduction

New babies can bring much joy. They also can bring worry. You may feel you don't know how to parent a baby. However, you can learn not only how to be a parent but also how to be a good parent. Paying attention to your baby is one way of learning to understand him and respond to his needs.

Another way to be a good parent involves learning about how babies develop. This book explains infant development from birth to age 1. All babies develop at their own pace. Your baby may be ahead of or behind the average age for a new skill. He still can be developing normally.

This book also teaches some basic infant cares. It is not, however, a replacement for a doctor's advice. You should talk with your baby's doctor if you have questions.

Attachment

Babies need to be held to feel safe. Hold your newborn as often as possible. Don't worry about spoiling her by holding her too much. Look into her eyes. Smile at her and talk with her often. Your baby will begin to trust you. Your future relationship will be stronger if you attach, or bond, to each other now.

DID YOU KNOW?

Some babies have a condition called colic. This is when they cry for long periods of time and cannot be comforted. Usually, babies with colic cry in the evening hours. Most babies outgrow colic in a few months. Check with your doctor if you think your baby is colicky.

COURTNEY, AGE 17

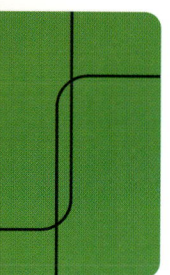

"When I brought my baby home, I held him all the time. My friends all wanted to hold him. But I just told them that he needed me, not them. My doctor said I did the right thing. She said that I had a healthier, happier baby because I paid a lot of attention to him. Now that he is a year old, I can tell he loves and trusts me."

Crying

Most newborns cry 2 to 3 hours or more each day. They cry for many reasons. Hunger cries usually are short and low-pitched. Some babies cry because they want to be left alone a short while. This cry is similar to the hunger cry. Angry cries seem more emotional. Pain or distress cries may include shrieking followed by a loud wail.

You can try many ways to calm your crying baby. You can feed him even if you don't think he should be hungry. The steady noise of running water, a vacuum cleaner, or a clothes dryer may soothe him. Your baby may prefer to be held while you walk around. Check that your baby isn't too warm or too cool. You also could take him for a car ride.

Your baby might need a different position. Try laying him on your arm and rubbing his back. Some babies like to lie across your knees with their tummy down. Rocking the baby in a rocking chair sometimes helps. You also can help by applying gentle pressure to his stomach. Keeping your baby upright for 20 minutes after a feeding may help, too.

Give yourself time away from a crying baby. Let someone whom you trust care for your baby for a while. Never shake your baby no matter how frustrated, angry, or sad you may become. Shaking can cause blindness, brain damage, and even death.

Helping Your Baby to Sleep

Newborns like to be snugly wrapped up in blankets. Lying on the back is the safest sleep position for babies, especially during the first 6 months. Lay your baby on a firm surface. Do not use pillows, quilts, or stuffed animals in the crib. They may block her airway. Babies should not be put to bed with a bottle.

Because she eats every few hours, your baby may not know the difference between night and day. You can teach her this difference. At night, keep feedings quiet, don't turn up the lights, and don't play with your baby. After a while, your baby should learn that nighttime is sleep time.

Health Watch

When changing your baby's diaper, expose her bottom to air as long as possible. This can help reduce the risk of diaper rash. It also may help to clear diaper rash that is already present.

Urination and Bowel Movements

Most newborns go through about 10 to 12 diapers each day. Change your baby's diaper after each feeding. This is a good time to check urination and bowel movements. Urination is the passing of liquid waste from the body. A bowel movement is the ridding of solid waste from the body. Your baby may urinate every 1 to 3 hours or, possibly, 4 to 6 times a day. He may have a bowel movement after each feeding. By 3 to 6 weeks, the number of bowel movements usually decreases for breastfed and formula-fed babies. They may have only one or up to several bowel movements per day.

A baby's first bowel movement usually is dark green or black. After the first few days, the stools change color. Breastfed babies have slightly runny stools that look like mustard with seeds in it. Formula-fed babies have tan or yellow stools that should be no firmer than peanut butter.

Diaper Rash

Diaper rash is a rash or irritation in the area the diaper covers. The most common cause is leaving a wet or dirty diaper on too long. Once a rash is present, it gets worse if not treated. To treat and reduce risk of diaper rash, change diapers as soon as possible after a bowel movement. Clean the area with a soft cloth and water after each bowel movement. Change wet diapers frequently. Talk with your doctor if the rash doesn't improve after a few days.

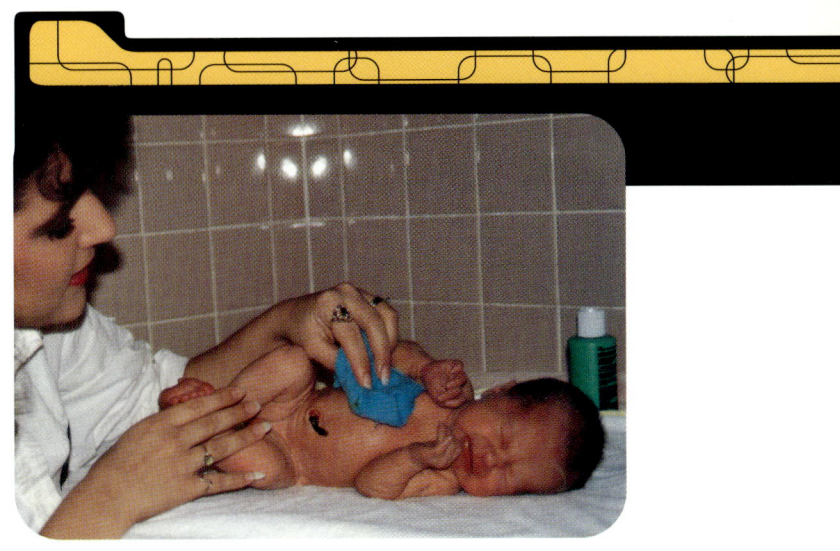

Bathing

Newborns don't need much bathing. Simply wash the diaper area well during diaper changes. Bathing too frequently can dry the skin. Give your baby only sponge baths until the umbilical cord falls off. This is the tube that connected the unborn baby to the mother's body. The cord is located in the belly button area.

To give a sponge bath, lay your baby somewhere flat and comfortable. Pad hard surfaces with a towel. Use a safety strap for areas above the floor. If a strap isn't used, constantly keep one hand on your baby to prevent a fall.

Have a basin of warm water and a basin of warm soapy water within reach. Put a washcloth in each basin. Keep your baby wrapped in a towel, and expose only the area you are washing. Use a damp cloth to wash your baby's face without soap. Then wash all the remaining body parts with the soapy washcloth. Rinse each body part with the rinse washcloth. Pay attention behind the ears and to armpits, folds in the neck, and the diaper area.

Once the umbilical cord falls off, you can place your baby directly in water. Many parents use the kitchen sink for the first few months. Put a towel down to avoid slips. Fill the sink with 2 inches or 5.1 centimeters of warm water. Always test the temperature with your elbow to make sure it isn't too warm. Place your baby in the water and support her head with one hand. Most of her body should be out of the water for safety. Use a plastic cup to pour water on her to keep her warm.

Begin by using a soft cloth to wash her face and hair. Cup your hand across her forehead when rinsing her head to protect her eyes. Wash and rinse the rest of her body from the top down. Keep your baby's head covered when she's wet, and dry her quickly so she doesn't get chilled. Never leave your baby alone in the bathtub. Take your baby with you if you must leave. Babies can drown in just a few inches or centimeters of water.

Cord, Nail, and Genital Care

The umbilical cord usually falls off 1 to 3 weeks after birth. Clean it once each day. Gently rub around the base of the cord with a cotton swab dipped in rubbing alcohol. Pull the cord up carefully with your fingers and gently push the swab into the base. This helps dry out the moist cord. Fold diapers down to keep the cord dry during the first few weeks. Call your baby's doctor if you notice a red area or bad smell.

Newborns' fingernails are very soft and difficult to cut. They may be sharp. You can file them gently the first few weeks until they harden. Then you can use a baby nail clipper.

Safety Tip

Find out how to set the water temperature in your home. It should be set at 120 degrees Fahrenheit (F) (48.9 degrees Celsius [C]). Then, if the water is accidentally turned on, it won't burn the baby.

Newborn girls sometimes have a discharge, or the release of a substance, from their vagina. The vagina is the passage that leads to the uterus where unborn babies develop. Simply wash a girl's genitals, or sex organs, from front to back.

Newborn boys often are circumcised. That means a doctor removed the foreskin, or a fold of skin at the head of the penis. The penis is the male sex organ. Clean the penis with plain water. Put a small dab of petroleum jelly on the tip with each diaper change. A yellow substance is normal on the tip of a healing circumcised penis. If you see blood, however, contact your doctor.

The uncircumcised penis can be cleaned simply with soap and water. Occasionally watch your baby urinate. Check to see that the hole in the foreskin is large enough to allow a urine stream.

Points to Consider

Why is it important to hold your baby as much as you can?

What are some reasons to change diapers often?

What can you do for diaper rash?

What might you do if the phone rings while you are giving your baby a bath?

Chapter Overview

- You can take steps to prevent common illnesses in your baby. Take your baby to the doctor for well-baby checkups and immunizations.

- You should never shake your baby. This can cause serious injury or death.

- Make your home a safe place for your baby to explore. Remove all safety hazards before he is old enough to get into them.

- Always use a safe infant car seat in the back center seat of the car.

- Choose a day care provider carefully. Ask many questions. Check references before you leave your baby with anyone.

Chapter 2

Health and Safety for Your New Baby

The job of keeping your baby safe and healthy is an ongoing one. This chapter discusses some health care and safety basics. For more information, see the book *Health Care for Infants and Toddlers* in this series.

Your Baby's Health

All babies get sick sooner or later. It is best to try to prevent your baby from getting sick in the first few months. During this time, his body may not fight off illness well. You can try the following to prevent common illnesses:

- **Have a close, loving relationship with your baby.** Less stress for your baby means fewer illnesses. Also, close attachment usually means you will recognize signs of illness quickly.

- **Feed your baby well and often.** See Chapter 3 for more information.

- **Keep germs away.** Friends and family are exposed to many cold and flu germs at school and work. Those germs can be dangerous for your baby. You can say politely that others can hold him when he is older. You can ask people to wash their hands with soap before holding your baby. Anyone who is ill should not come near him.

- **Don't let anyone smoke around your baby.** Babies who are exposed to cigarette smoke have a higher rate of many illnesses than do other babies.

- **Take your baby to well-baby checkups and get his immunizations, or shots.** Well-baby checkups are scheduled appointments with your baby's doctor. This schedule is listed below. The schedule sometimes changes, so check with your doctor to be sure.

Doctor Visits

Your baby should go to the doctor when 2 to 4 days old. He also should go at ages 1 month, 2 months, 4 months, 6 months, 9 months, and 12 months. At these checkups, your baby's doctor will give him immunizations. These shots protect your baby from serious diseases. It is important to get these shots at the right ages, when they are most effective.

Taking Your Baby's Temperature

Sometimes your baby may seem very warm. He may have a fever. Use a rectal thermometer to take your baby's temperature. Before taking his temperature, try to calm your baby. Always shake down a bulb thermometer to below 96 degrees Fahrenheit (F) (35.6 degrees Celsius [C]) before beginning.

Health Watch

All babies spit up at some time or another. But if your baby's spit up is forceful or extreme, call your doctor.

Lay your baby on a flat surface. He should be either on his back with his legs up or on his stomach. Gently spread his buttocks. This is the fleshy body part where one sits. Insert a thermometer that is lubricated, or slippery with petroleum jelly, 1 inch (2.5 centimeters) into the rectum. This opening marks the ending of the intestine. Don't push too far, and don't let go. Glass thermometers can be read in 3 minutes. Digital thermometers can be read in 30 seconds. The average rectal temperature is 99.6 degrees F (37.6 degrees C).

Call your doctor if your baby is:

- 2 months or younger and has a rectal temperature of 100.4 degrees F (38 degrees C) or higher

- 3 to 6 months old and has a rectal temperature of 101 degrees F (38.3 degrees C) or higher

- Older than 6 months and has a rectal temperature of 103 degrees F (39.4 degrees C) or higher

Lowering Your Baby's Fever

There are several ways to help lower your baby's fever.

- **Give your baby acetaminophen or ibuprofen.** Do not give aspirin because it has been linked to a serious condition called Reye Syndrome. Follow your doctor's recommendation for how much acetaminophen or ibuprofen to give your baby. The dose of these medicines depends on her weight.

SAFETY TIP

Never allow your baby to play with plastic grocery-type bags or balloons in any form. These could cause choking or strangulation.

- **Keep the environment cool.** Do not put too many clothes on a baby who has a fever.
- **Feed the fever.** If your baby is eating solids, offer extra liquids and solids. If you are nursing or bottlefeeding, offer feedings often.
- **Put your baby in a lukewarm, or slightly warm, bath.**

Baby Safety

There are many situations in which you have to take steps to help keep your baby safe.

Unsafe Environments

Babies learn to wiggle and roll before you know it. You never know how early your baby will start moving. Therefore, you should never leave her alone on a high surface. This is true even if she is sitting in an infant seat or carrier. Always move your baby to a safe place or take her with you.

It is important not to leave your baby alone with an unfit caregiver. If you feel someone is not safe for your baby, do not leave her with that person.

Sudden Infant Death Syndrome

Sudden Infant Death Syndrome (SIDS) is the sudden, unexplainable death of an infant younger than 1 year of age. Most often, SIDS occurs to babies within 6 months. It occurs most commonly between midnight and 6 A.M. The cause of SIDS is unknown. Recently, experts have found a connection between sleep position and SIDS. Therefore, doctors urge that babies be put down to sleep on their back. Your baby should sleep on his back unless your doctor tells you otherwise.

Child Abuse and Neglect

Sometimes parents get so upset with babies that they shake or hit them. This is dangerous. You should never shake or hit your baby. It could result in death or serious injury. It is better to put your baby down and let her cry. Explain this to anyone who cares for your baby.

If you feel you are at risk for abusing your baby, get help right away. Your doctor can provide the names and phone numbers of therapists and social workers. These people can help you safely cope with your problems. Never abandon your baby. If you feel you need to get away, leave her with someone you trust.

Baby-Proofing Your Home

Home should be a safe place for babies to explore. Creating a safe home can avoid possible injuries to your baby such as poisoning, choking, electrocution, and other dangers.

FRANK, AGE 17

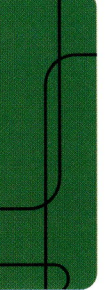

"The early childhood education teacher said to remove as many no's as possible. We did this. We put all my mom's sewing stuff up high. We faced the CD holder to the wall. We gave all our plants to my grandpa for a while. Now we don't have to say no to my baby very often. I'm glad she can explore without somebody stopping her all the time."

SAFETY TIP

Do not use infant seats or infant carriers in place of infant car seats.

Look at every room in which your baby spends time. Remove anything she can choke on or be strangled by. Tie up cords from window blinds and curtains. Make sure your baby's crib is away from windows with cords. Give plants away or put them up high. Use safety gates for all stairways. Lock poisonous substances, cleaners, and firearms out of reach. Use outlet covers, drawer and cabinet locks, and stove-knob covers. Have your home checked for lead paint.

Traveling in the Car With Your Baby

Always use an infant car seat when traveling in the car with your baby. Use one that meets government safety standards. Always follow the instructions for installation. The safest place for your baby is in the back center seat. Never use any car seat in the front seat of cars with an airbag. Choose a car seat appropriate for your baby's age and weight.

Choosing a Day Care Provider

You'll probably need a day care provider during school or work. Grandparents may or may not be the best care providers. Whomever you choose, avoid someone who smokes. Also, check references of anyone you interview.

Before deciding, visit the care provider's home or center. Spend time watching that person with children. What does he or she do when they cry? Is the person sensitive? How does she or he discipline children? Does the person hold the babies often? Does the person seem to enjoy the work? How do the children seem around the caregiver? After you feel comfortable with a candidate, let that person hold your baby to observe them together. Then, you may want to give care with that person a test run.

Points to Consider

Your friend's 2-year-old son has a cold. They want to visit you and your baby. What would you say?

Why should you never shake a baby? What are some things you can do if you are upset with your baby?

What might you do if your baby comes home from day care smelling like cigarette smoke?

Chapter Overview

- Doctors recommend breastfeeding for newborn babies. Positioning is important when breastfeeding. Breastfed newborns eat every 1½ to 3 hours.

- Bottlefed newborns eat every 3 to 4 hours. Mix formula according to directions. Never prop your baby with a bottle.

- As babies get older, they eat more at each feeding with more time between feedings.

- Babies may or may not need extra breast milk or formula to drink during hot weather. Give juice only if solids have been introduced.

- It is important to burp your baby often. There are several ways to do this.

Chapter 3

Breastfeeding and Bottlefeeding

Most doctors recommend breastfeeding, or nursing, for newborn babies. The milk a mother's body provides is the best nutrition for babies. Nursing helps a baby and its mother to feel close. Some women choose not to breastfeed their babies. Babies still can get good nutrition even if they are not breastfed.

Breastfeeding

A female's breasts produce colostrum for a few days after she gives birth. This thin, yellow fluid protects the baby against many diseases. Real milk is produced after a few days. Then, breasts might feel full and uncomfortable. Some milk can be squeezed out with the fingers for relief. The fullness should lessen in a few days.

Preparing to Breastfeed

The mother should find a calm, comfortable place to nurse. Milk will "let down" only after relaxation. The mother massages her breasts with the palm of her hand before beginning. This is done by holding the nipple between the thumb and index finger to form a **C**. The mother then rubs her nipple on the baby's lips with her free hand. This gets the baby to open his mouth. The baby's knees, chest, and nose should touch the mother. When the baby's mouth opens, the mother gently pulls the baby toward her breast.

Positioning is important to breastfeeding success. Good positioning means the baby can latch on the right way. This reduces the risk of the mother's nipples getting sore or cracked. It is wise to switch positions often. A lactation consultant can teach more about positioning and give other advice on breastfeeding. Most hospitals have a lactation consultant on staff. Before leaving the hospital, ask to talk with one. Your doctor also can tell you how to get in touch with one.

How Much to Feed Your Baby

Your baby will determine how often nursing is needed in the beginning. Newborns nurse about every 1½ to 3 hours. Feeding her baby when he wants to eat can build up the mother's milk supply. The mother's body makes milk according to how much her baby sucks. A mother may have to wake her baby if he falls asleep during nursing. She can do this by removing the baby's clothing or by tickling his feet.

As your baby grows, he will nurse longer at each feeding. Then feedings will begin to be further apart. By 6 weeks, he probably will nurse every 2 to 3 hours. There will be a longer period between feedings at night. By the time your baby is 12 pounds (5.4 kilograms) or more, he may sleep 6 hours at night without nursing.

Fast Fact

Caffeine, onions, broccoli, and cabbage in your diet could make your breastfed baby fussy. Caffeine is a drug that stimulates a person. If your baby cries a lot, try eliminating these items from your diet.

Babies usually nurse 10 to 20 minutes on each breast during a feeding. They should be burped after every 5 to 10 minutes. A baby nurses longest on the first breast. Then, the mother offers the second breast until the baby is finished. You'll know the baby is finished when he acts uninterested. The mother starts the next feeding on the breast where her baby last nursed.

Supplemental Bottles

Breastfeeding alone is best for the first 3 to 4 weeks. But the mother may need to introduce a bottle so she can go to school or work. The supplemented, or added, bottle contains either formula or breast milk that has been expressed from the mother's breasts. Expressing milk means gently squeezing it out. The mother should continue to breastfeed her baby when she is with him. This helps to keep up the mother's milk supply.

Storing and Thawing Breast Milk

Breast milk can be stored for 2 days in the refrigerator. This is true if the refrigerator's temperature is between 32 and 39 degrees F (0 and 3.9 degrees C). Breast milk can be kept up to 2 weeks in a freezer. The milk can be kept 3 to 4 months if the freezer door is separate from the refrigerator door.

CHAPTER 3 ■ BREASTFEEDING AND BOTTLEFEEDING

Did You Know?

For help with breastfeeding, you can contact the La Leche League in your area. This worldwide organization helps families learn about and enjoy breastfeeding. Check the *For More Information* section at the back of this book for contact information.

Never thaw breast milk in the microwave. This destroys some of the milk's nutrients, or healthy substances. Milk thawed in the microwave could burn your baby. Instead, place the frozen container in a bowl of warm water for a few minutes. This process quickly thaws milk. Once thawed, use the milk within 24 hours. Do not refreeze it.

Tina, Age 18

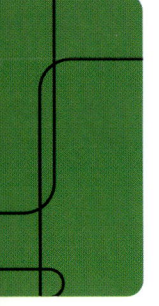

"I decided to breastfeed my baby because my sister had breastfed her daughter. At first, it hurt a lot. It was messy, and I was always tired. There were so many reasons to quit. But I knew it was best for my baby's health for at least the first 6 months. I'm glad I stuck with it that long. My baby is very healthy. Plus, I have a bond with him that no one else could ever have."

Bottlefeeding

Your baby's doctor can help you choose the best formula for your baby. It is important to follow the directions on the package exactly. Always store prepared formula in the refrigerator. If the formula isn't used within 24 hours, throw it out. Also, throw out any formula the baby does not drink from the bottle. Bacteria could grow in it and cause sickness.

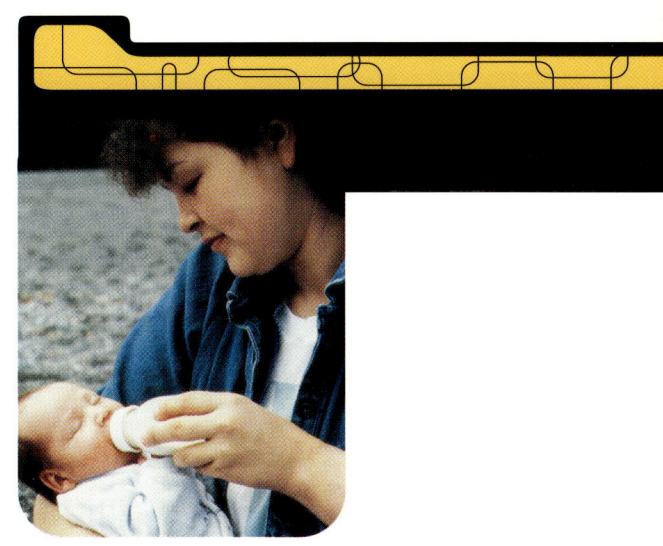

Most babies prefer formula warmed. You should not microwave formula. The microwaved formula could burn your baby. You can hold the bottle under warm running tap water to warm it. You also can place it in a bowl of warm water. Always test the formula's temperature on the inside of your wrist. Then you can be sure the formula isn't too warm.

Feeding With the Bottle

Find a chair where you can prop your arms as you feed your baby. Hold him in a semi-upright position. Hold the bottle so that formula covers the nipple of the bottle. This prevents your baby from swallowing too much air. Stroke the bottle against your baby's lower lip or cheek to get him to begin sucking. Never leave your baby with a propped bottle. He could choke or develop ear infections or tooth decay.

How Much and How Often to Feed Your Baby

Your newborn probably will take 2 to 3 ounces (59.1 to 88.7 milliliters) of formula per feeding. He will eat every 3 to 4 hours during the first few weeks. Wake him to eat if he sleeps longer than 5 hours during the first month. At the end of the first month, he should take around 4 ounces (118.3 milliliters) per feeding about every 4 hours. By 6 months, he will take 6 to 8 ounces (177.4 to 236.6 milliliters) 4 or 5 times every 24 hours. These are guidelines. Your baby's amounts and times will vary from day to day.

Health Watch

Some babies need extra iron and fluoride during their first year. Fluoride is a chemical that helps prevent tooth decay. Formula-fed babies usually don't need supplements. They drink iron-fortified formula and get fluoride from the water used to mix formula. Breastfed babies may need supplements after 6 months. Check with your baby's doctor.

Water and Juice

Babies usually get all needed water from breast milk or formula. During very hot weather, you can offer more frequent feedings. Infants should not be given plain water. Their body cannot handle it yet.

Use fruit juice only when your baby starts solids. Begin by mixing half juice and half water. Avoid orange juice until your baby is at least 6 months old. Offer your baby no more than 4 ounces (118.3 milliliters) per day until she is a year old. Check with your doctor about giving your baby extra liquids when she is ill.

Burping, Hiccuping, and Spitting Up

Babies feel pain when they swallow air during a feeding. Burp your baby frequently even if she doesn't show discomfort. This pause in eating and change of position slows gulping. It also reduces the amount of air taken in. Bottlefed babies usually burp every 2 to 3 ounces (59.1 to 88.7 milliliters). Breastfed babies usually burp every 5 to 10 minutes.

Here are three techniques for burping your baby. You will soon realize which works best for your baby.

- Hold your baby upright with her head on your shoulder. Support her head and back with one hand. Gently but firmly pat her back with your other hand.

- Lay the baby on her stomach on your lap. Support her head so it is higher than her chest. Gently but firmly pat or rub your hand on her back.

- Set the baby on your lap. Support her chest and head with one hand. Gently but firmly pat her back with your other hand.

Many babies hiccup. Hiccups usually do not bother babies. However, if your baby is feeding, the hiccups may be bothersome. Change your baby's position. Try to get her to burp or relax. Wait until the hiccups are gone to continue feeding.

Many babies spit up frequently. Most are out of this phase by the time they can sit up. Some continue through their first year. To decrease the amount of spitting up, try these tips:

- Make feeding time peaceful.
- Burp your bottlefed baby at least every 3 to 5 minutes.
- Do not feed your baby while she is lying down.
- Keep your baby upright for 20 minutes after feeding.
- Try to feed your baby before she is extremely hungry to avoid gulping.
- Decrease the amount you feed your baby.
- Don't play roughly with your baby immediately after feeding.

HEALTH WATCH

Never lay your baby flat to feed. This could cause choking or ear infections.

POINTS TO CONSIDER

How often should a newborn baby be breastfed? How often should a newborn be bottlefed?

What could you do if your sister warms your baby's formula in the microwave?

Why should you dump leftover formula from the bottle after your baby finishes feeding?

If your baby seems warm during a summertime picnic, should you give him water? Explain.

Chapter Overview

- Solid foods can be introduced around 6 months. Continue bottlefeeding or breastfeeding through your baby's first year.

- Use foods that are especially prepared for babies.

- In the beginning, babies eat only tiny amounts of solid foods.

Chapter 4

Introducing Solids

When Is the Right Time to Introduce Solids?

Most doctors say that your baby should begin solids somewhere around 6 months. Watch for these signs of readiness. Your baby:

- Sits with support, reaches and grabs, and puts most things in her mouth
- Watches with interest as you eat
- Reaches for your food
- Doesn't push her tongue out as frequently as she used to
- Opens her mouth when you open yours to eat
- Seems to be eating more and more often for several days
- Opens her mouth when offered food and does not turn away

What Foods Do I Start With?

Make sure to use foods that are prepared especially for babies. Begin with single-grain rice cereal mixed with breast milk or formula. Follow the directions on the box. Some nursing mothers begin with mashed bananas because breastfed babies are used to breast milk's sweet taste.

After your baby has adjusted to those foods, try mashed carrots, sweet potatoes, and squash. Next try pears, applesauce, peaches, or prunes. These baby foods are the easiest to digest. Some experts believe vegetables should be started before fruits. Otherwise, babies may like sweet tastes too much. Fruits also can cause diarrhea more often than vegetables do. This is a condition in which normally solid waste become runny and frequent.

Later, you can try most other baby foods. To start, feed only one food at a time. To watch for signs of food sensitivity, allow 3 days before introducing a new food. If a baby does not tolerate a food, she may be gassy or fussy. She may have diarrhea or a skin rash around the lips.

Many parents like to begin feeding solids with their fingers instead of a spoon. Touch the food to your baby's lips. She may make funny faces because the taste is so new. This doesn't mean she isn't ready. Some babies have not learned how to keep their tongue in their mouth. This means they aren't able to push the food back to the throat.

SAFETY TIP

To prevent allergies and botulism, or food poisoning, do not give your baby these foods until age 3:

Peanuts or peanut butter

Eggs

Tomatoes

Shellfish

Honey

Your baby may show you she isn't ready by turning away or pursing her lips. Try again in a week. Remember that you are only introducing solids. Your baby's main nutrition still comes from formula or breast milk. Solid foods should make up only 50 percent of her diet by her first birthday.

MIGUEL, AGE 17

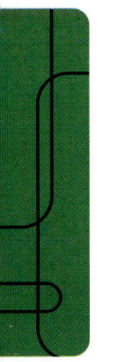

"Sometimes feeding Leo can be tiring. He's messy, and food gets all over the place. Sometimes the food even ends up on me. But feeding time can be fun, too. The first time I fed Leo some applesauce, he made the funniest face. I wished my girlfriend had had the camera out. About a week later, we tried to give Leo applesauce again. Sheila had the camera ready this time. Instead of making a face, Leo ate it. Now applesauce is one of his regular foods."

Did You Know?

Your baby will choose the correct amount to eat. A baby stops eating when her stomach is full.

How Much and How Often Do I Feed My Baby?

At first, you'll feed your baby solids only once a day. Begin by offering only a spoonful or two. Gradually increase the amount to a quarter cup (59.1 milliliters) or more at a time. Pay attention to the signs that your baby has had enough. She may turn away, seem disinterested, or purse her lips. That means it's time to quit even if she has had only a few bites. Some days, she may refuse to eat anything at all. This is normal.

Feed new foods in the morning. Otherwise, offer solids when your baby seems hungriest or bored. Choose a time of day when you are not stressed. Babies are messy and slow eaters. Eventually, you'll feed your baby solids every time you sit down for a meal. By then, you should offer your baby about 4 ounces (118.3 milliliters) of strained baby food at each meal. If your baby rejects a food, try it again in a week or two.

Continuing With Solid Foods

By 7 to 9 months, your baby can pick up objects with his thumb and forefinger. That means you can introduce finger foods. You must be very careful about choking at this stage. Avoid hard crunchy foods such as raw vegetables and nuts. Instead, offer foods that melt easily in the mouth and do not require chewing.

By 9 months, offer these foods:

- Cooked carrot pieces
- Unsweetened, O-shaped cereals
- Mashed potatoes
- Teething biscuits
- Well-cooked, cut-up green beans, peas, and potatoes
- Rice-cake pieces
- ¼ inch (.6 centimeter) cubes of cheese
- ¼ inch (.6 centimeter) cubes of soft fruits

Around 1 year of age, your baby may want to feed herself with a spoon. Let her do this whenever possible. You may hold the spoon when she grabs on. At this stage, it is best to offer thicker foods that will stick to the spoon. Refer to the chart on the next page for guidelines on what foods to offer at which ages.

Baby Foods and Their Appropriate Age for Introduction

4 to 7 months	7 to 9 months	9 to 12 months
Breast milk/formula	Breast milk/formula	Breast milk/formula
Bananas	Mashed potatoes	Peas
Rice cereal	Pears	Papaya
Sweet potatoes	Applesauce	Refried beans
	Carrots	Cheese
	Squash	Yogurt
	Avocados	Oatmeal
	Teething biscuits	Rice cakes
	Peaches	Lamb
	Prunes	Poultry
	Barley cereal	Rice pasta
		Apricots

POINTS TO CONSIDER

What are some signs your baby is ready for solid foods?

What are the best solids to begin with?

What does it mean if your baby makes a face the first time you feed her cooked carrots?

How can you keep track of possible food sensitivities?

Chapter Overview

- Your baby's neck, stomach, and leg muscles are getting stronger. He may be able to roll over. Your baby needs the chance to develop his muscles.

- Your baby likes to look at your face. Smile often at him. Make exaggerated facial expressions.

- Talk often with your baby. Imitate the sounds you hear him make. Take turns making noises. This can encourage your baby to begin talking.

- By 3 months, many babies sleep 7 or 8 hours without waking.

Chapter 5

Your Baby: 1 to 3 Months

Physical Changes

Your baby's muscles may seem to get stronger each day. She may be able to roll over, even if you don't know it. This is why you must never leave her alone on a high surface. The following activities help muscle development and are ways of playing with your baby at this early stage.

- **To develop neck muscles:** give your baby time on the floor on her tummy.

- **To develop stomach muscles:** gently pull her up by her arms from a lying position to a sitting position.

- **To develop leg strength:** try to lift her from a sitting position to an upright position with her feet on the floor. Hold your hands around her stomach and back.

- **To develop hand and arm muscles:** offer your baby a small rattle to grasp.

Safety Tip

Never allow anyone, including yourself, to smoke around your baby.

Never hold your baby while eating or drinking anything hot or while cooking.

Seeing and Hearing

At 1 month, your baby cannot see more than 12 inches (30.5 centimeters) away. Look at him close up. Play facial games with him. Imitate his facial expressions. Smile often. Use exaggerated facial gestures with your eyes open wide. Babies love to look at faces, especially their parents' faces. You may see your baby's first real smile during this stage.

By 3 months, your baby may see you halfway across a room. Try not to let your baby watch television. Instead, offer contrasting bright and dark objects to look at. Babies enjoy looking at mobiles that hang above them. Black and white contrast is especially interesting to babies during this stage.

Babies prefer high-pitched tones. Talk with your baby often. This helps him to learn the importance of speech. At 1 month, he can recognize your voice. He is comforted by it, so talk often. Even talk with him when you are in another room.

Reading to your baby is another way to stimulate him. It also can help you and your baby bond.

Allison, Age 15

"I can tell my baby likes to see me and hear my voice. She is almost 5 weeks old. When she sees my face, she lights up. I think she'll smile soon. I usually lay her near me when I do my homework on the floor. I read my lessons out loud. Sometimes I use silly voices. She stares at me for a long time. I know she feels safe when she hears my voice. The cool thing is that I think I am learning more by saying some of my homework out loud!"

Language Development

Imitating the sounds you hear your baby make can help her language skills. Another way to help is to take turns "talking." Mix baby talk with adult talk. Do this so your baby can learn adult sounds. She probably will not babble until 4 or 5 months. Babbling is when your baby makes gibberish sounds that resemble language. However, you always should talk with her because babies can understand language before they can speak it.

Social and Emotional Development

Your baby will learn trust if you meet her needs early in life. Hold her often. Go to her when she cries. Experts recommend that you meet your baby's needs quickly during the first 6 months. Those experts believe that babies then will be less demanding when they're older.

Sleeping

By 3 months, many babies sleep 7 or 8 hours without waking. If your baby does not do this, you may try keeping him awake longer during the evening. Play actively at these times. Increase the amount of feeding just before bed. This can help him to not wake up hungry.

Some babies get days and nights mixed up at this age. If this happens, keep your baby awake as long as possible in the evening. If he does wake up at night, keep the lights low. Don't talk or play with him.

Many parents think their baby wakes up too early in the morning. You might try dark shades on the window. You might keep him up an extra hour at night. When he is older, try keeping a few safe toys in the crib for when he wakes. Do not use stuffed toys, however. Your baby could suffocate on them. You could try letting your baby fuss for a bit to see if he will go back to sleep.

At a Glance

By the end of 3 months, your baby should be able to:

Smile at the sound of your voice

Begin to imitate some sounds

Turn her head toward the direction of a sound

Marcus, Age 17

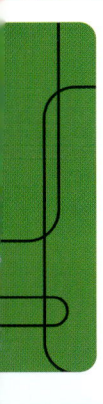

"Before my baby was born, I slept in until 8:30 A.M. and could still get to school by 9:15. Then we had our baby. She used to wake up at about 5:00. We kept her up an extra hour at night. That seemed to help. Now she sleeps a little later. We still need to get up at 6:00 or 7:00 every day, even weekends! I just go to bed earlier now. It feels weird to go to bed so early. But at least I'm less tired and crabby with my daughter in the morning. It makes me a better dad."

Points to Consider

Which is better: letting your baby watch television or showing him pictures and objects from around the house? Why?

Why is it important that you talk with your baby?

What should you do if your baby has his days and nights mixed up?

Chapter Overview

- During this stage, babies usually grasp things, roll over, and sit up. They need time on their tummy. They also need help to practice sitting. By 6 to 8 months, most babies sit without help. Babies also bring objects to their mouth during this stage. To avoid possible choking, keep small objects away.

- Help to stimulate your baby by carrying him around the house and naming things out loud. Let your baby look in the mirror often. Babies in this stage begin to understand cause and effect.

- Most babies this age sleep through the night. Usually, they can go at least 9 hours at night without a feeding.

- Babies usually begin teething during this stage. Teeth may appear as early as 4 months. Or, they may not appear until much later.

- When your baby is around 7 months old, you can discourage negative behavior and reward desired behavior.

Chapter 6

Your Baby: 4 to 7 Months

Physical Changes

During this stage, babies usually grasp things, roll over, and sit up. They may even crawl. Your baby now will choose what she wants to do and try to do it.

Your baby may be able to raise her head. She may hold it up while lying on her stomach. Once she can do that, she can begin lifting her chest with her arms. She also may rock on her stomach. These skills are necessary for rolling over. Give your baby time on her tummy.

Let your baby practice sitting up once she can raise her chest off the ground. Hold her or support her with pillows as she learns to balance herself. Soon she may sit with both hands on the floor. Put bright toys in front of her to look at while she learns balance. By 6 to 8 months, your baby should be able to sit alone. It is important to give her help and practice sitting.

Did You Know?

Use the words *hi* and *hello* or your baby's name to begin conversations with him. This helps him to focus on the conversation. He will learn that it's time to talk with you.

Your baby will bring objects to her mouth during this stage. Give your baby safe objects to hold. Keep small objects away to avoid choking.

Your baby will discover body parts she didn't know about. She will play with her toes and feet. She even might put them in her mouth. She may touch her genitals during a diaper change. You can teach your baby about her body by naming the parts she touches.

Seeing and Hearing

Your baby now can follow most movements. Show him red and blue objects. Those colors are interesting to babies at this stage. Your baby soon will be able to grab moving things. At 5 months, babies are bored with mobiles. If your baby is sitting up, remove any mobiles so he doesn't grab them. He could choke or strangle himself.

Help to stimulate your baby by carrying him around the house and naming things out loud. Let your baby look in the mirror often. Babies love to look at themselves.

Language Development

At 4 months, your baby may start to babble. Encourage your baby to talk by repeating sounds that you hear him make. Talk with your doctor if your baby doesn't imitate sounds by the seventh month. It may mean a problem with hearing or speech development.

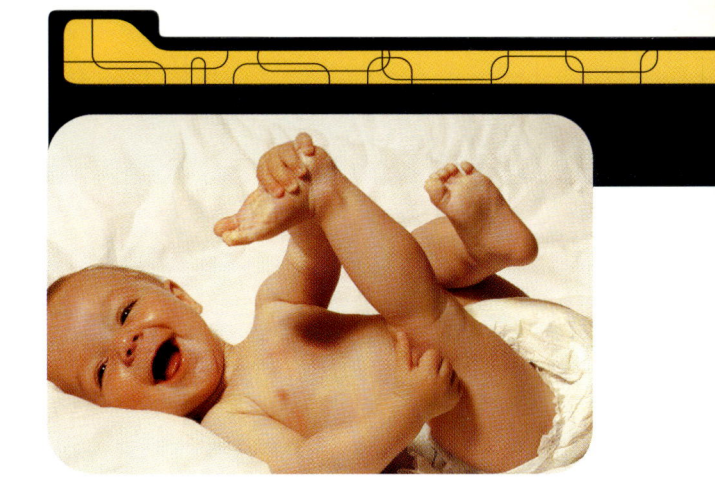

Social and Emotional Development

Babies in this stage begin to understand cause and effect. For example, your baby may realize that toys make noise when shaken. She may learn to drop things to see you pick them up. She may wait for you to say "bless you" when she sneezes. Babies often smile when things happen that they expect to happen.

Safe, cheap toy choices include wooden spoons and unbreakable cups. Lids and boxes also are good choices. Many babies this age like to play with empty pie tins. Playing peek-a-boo with your baby is fun for her at this stage as well.

Your baby's personality becomes apparent during this stage. Headstrong babies easily get upset, so extra patience is needed with them. Some babies seem content when instead they really are scared or shy. Quiet babies often need extra encouragement. During this stage, your baby may smile at strangers and give them attention. This is a good time to introduce your baby to future baby-sitters.

Your baby may be very vocal about her needs. She may cry to let you know she is bored with a toy. She may scream with excitement to keep playing a game. She may cry when you leave the room because she is attached to you and feels safe with you.

Sleeping

Babies this age should be able to go at least 9 hours at night without a feeding. Most babies still need two naps each day. The naps may be from 1 to 3 hours in the morning and the afternoon. This isn't always the case. Some babies take short half-hour naps several times each day. Let your baby sleep as long as he needs to when he naps. Do this unless he has trouble falling asleep at night.

Some babies have trouble falling asleep at night. Having a routine helps to calm babies. Try to do the same thing each evening. This may mean a bath and a story. You might try soft music. You may rock your baby or nurse or bottlefeed him. These activities can soothe your baby. They help him know it's time to sleep.

It is best to put your baby in his crib before he falls asleep. This helps him learn to fall asleep on his own. Try patting his back and quietly talking with him before leaving the room. Experts disagree on whether to let a baby cry himself to sleep. Some say you shouldn't let your baby cry. They believe it teaches the baby not to trust you. They also believe it makes the baby anxious.

Did You Know?

When teething, babies often wake up at night. Many doctors recommend using a dose of acetaminophen before bedtime for teething babies to help them sleep. Check with your doctor about the correct dosage for your baby's weight.

The American Academy of Pediatrics (AAP) recommends letting your baby cry 5 minutes before responding. Then, go in to comfort him for 1 minute without picking him up. Tell your baby you love him and then leave. Wait another 5 minutes and repeat the steps as needed. Check crying that goes on for 20 minutes. Something could be wrong. For example, the baby might be ill.

The AAP also recommends letting your baby cry a few minutes during the night. He may fall back asleep. When you do go in, make it short. Rub his back. If that doesn't work, cuddle him. Do not, however, bring him to your bed. Do not feed him unless you believe he is hungry. If you do these things, he may expect them each night and may not sleep without them.

Teething

Babies usually begin teething during this age. Teeth usually appear sometime around the fourth month. Sometimes it is much later. Usually, the two bottom front teeth are the first to appear, followed by the two top front teeth. Teething can be painful to babies. They may be irritable and drool a lot. Some babies run a low fever (not over 100 degrees F [37.8 degrees C]).

Teething babies often want to chew on something hard. Give your baby firm rubber teething rings. Try rubbing her gums with your clean finger. Don't put teething rings in the freezer. This makes them too hard and can hurt your baby.

When teeth do come in, make a habit of cleaning them. Gently brush them at the end of the day. Use a soft baby toothbrush or a soft washcloth. Never let your baby fall asleep with a bottle. This helps prevent future cavities.

Behavior Changes and Positive Discipline

Your baby will begin to show interest in many things. Some of those things may be dangerous for him. Your baby cannot misbehave on purpose at this age. He won't understand if you punish him or raise your voice. Instead, be calm, firm, and loving. It is best to distract him with another toy or activity at this stage. His memory doesn't allow him to remember what you've taught him.

LING, AGE 16

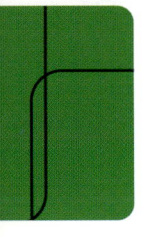

"We try to be very specific when we tell my 7-month-old what he can't do. My aunt's house, where we live, has radiators. We tell my baby 'Don't touch the radiator,' instead of just 'Don't touch.' That way, he knows it's okay to touch some things but not others."

At a Glance

By the end of 7 months, your baby should be able to:

Respond to her own name

Tell the difference in your emotion by your tone of voice

Use her voice to express happiness and unhappiness

Babble in chains of sounds, such as "baa, bee, boo, bee, baa"

Respond to sounds by making sounds

When your baby is around 7 months old, you can begin discouraging negative behavior. Most doctors do not believe in spanking. Babies do not understand being punished or spanked. They do not know what a raised voice means. It is best to reward desired behavior. For example, cuddle and thank your baby for being gentle if he fingers your hair. If he pulls your hair, let him know it is wrong. Calmly say "no pulling" while you stop his pulling. Use an activity or toy for distraction.

Points to Consider

Why should you give your baby time on his tummy and practice sitting up?

What are some inexpensive toy choices for your baby at this stage?

Why should you put your baby in his crib before he is asleep?

What would you say to your baby if you saw her about to touch a light socket?

Chapter Overview

- At 8 months, your baby probably can sit without support. She even may begin crawling between 7 and 10 months. She might learn to go up and down stairs during this stage. She even may begin walking.

- Babies in this stage learn to use their thumb and first or second fingers to pick up things. Then your baby will begin to drop and throw things.

- Some babies begin talking around their first birthday.

- Most babies develop anxiety around strangers and anxiety about separating from parents during this stage.

Chapter 7

Your Baby: 8 to 12 Months

Physical Changes

At 8 months, your baby probably can sit without support. Soon she may lean over to pick up toys. She will figure out how to get onto her stomach and return to a sitting position. Most babies this age do not stop moving for very long. Never leave your baby alone on a high surface. She could fall off and be seriously hurt.

Babies usually begin crawling between 7 and 10 months. Most babies begin by rocking on their hands and knees. Some go backward before they go forward. Some children never do crawl. This is okay as long as your baby scoots or twists to get around. Placing objects just out of her reach may encourage her to crawl.

Your baby probably will learn to use stairs during this stage. Never allow her to do this alone. Use safety gates to keep your baby away from stairs. Teach her to go down steps backward. Practice only on the first few steps. It's best if the steps are carpeted. Your baby probably will tumble many times before learning this skill.

Walking

Most babies take their first steps around their first birthday. Some are much later or earlier. Your baby will begin by pulling himself up to a standing position. He'll need help learning how to get back down. Gently bend his knees to lower him to the ground. Next, he'll begin to walk along furniture. Make sure your furniture has no sharp edges.

Soon, he'll let go of his hold on furniture for a few moments at a time. In time, your baby will take maybe one or two steps before dropping. Eventually, he'll walk on his own. Babies who begin to walk need shoes to protect their feet. Look for comfortable shoes with nonskid soles.

Gayle, Age 17

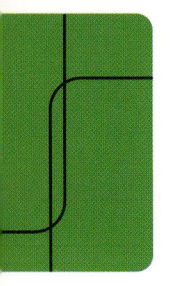

"My 14-month-old, April, isn't walking yet. My friend's baby walked at 9 months. I guess it's nothing to worry about. April takes a few steps around furniture. Sometimes she takes a few steps toward my mom or me when we hold our arms out. But April's just not ready to walk on her own. Her doctor says she'll do it when she's ready."

SAFETY TIP

Never use a piece of baby equipment called a walker. The AAP says that walkers do not encourage babies to walk on their own. The AAP also says that walkers can be a safety hazard.

Using Fingers

Your baby will learn to use his thumb and first or second fingers to pick up things. Then he will begin to drop and throw things. Make sure you give him soft toys to play with. He may bang the toys on his head. Play with your baby by giving him toys to drop. He will enjoy seeing you pick up the objects he drops.

Babies this age like things with moving parts. Give your baby toys with levers, wheels, and doors. Stack blocks so your baby can tip them over. By the end of this period, your baby will begin to stack his own block towers.

Language Development

Some babies begin talking around their first birthday. Most babies only say syllables such as "baa," "gee," "daa," "maa," and "mee." This means they are getting ready to talk. Help your baby learn to talk by telling her what you are doing. Use simple language. For example say, "You are in the water," or "What a soft blanket."

The more you talk with your baby, the better. In this stage, your baby begins to understand more of what you say. This is true even though she cannot say the words herself.

At a Glance

Try these suggestions to help your baby separate from you:

Spend a few minutes with your baby when you drop him off.

Never sneak out. Instead, tell your baby you are leaving.

Tell your baby when you are leaving and then go.

Always tell your baby you will be back for him.

Make sure your baby is well-rested and fed before leaving him with others.

Mama or *Dada* is often a first word babies use. Pay attention to your baby so you can recognize her first words. She may say "bee" for blanket. Still call words by their proper name. This helps teach your baby the right way to say them.

Experts recommend teaching babies this age some basic sign language to communicate with before they can talk. Some practical words are *drink, eat, up, down,* and *book*. Teaching these signs can reduce frustration, or discouragement, for babies and parents. It also can cut down on whining. Parents can make up the signs.

Social and Emotional Development

Babies this age are curious. Your baby's new ability to move helps him to explore new things. He'll probably pull objects out of drawers and off shelves whenever possible. Keep an eye on your baby when he is exploring. Make sure nothing unsafe is in his path.

Your baby is learning that things continue to exist even when they are out of sight. Peek-a-boo is a fun game at this stage. Another game involves letting your baby see you hide a toy in an obvious place. He will probably go to find it.

Babies at this stage often enjoy toys made out of ordinary household objects. Offer your baby wooden spoons, plastic lids, plastic containers, and other safe objects. When he is bored with a toy, make a small change to it. For example, you can put a block inside a plastic container with the lid on. Your baby can now shake the container.

Your baby may develop anxiety, or fear, around strangers and anxiety about separating from you. He may cry when you leave the room and at bedtime. When you leave him with someone else, he may scream. These anxieties usually happen between 10 and 18 months. Some parents feel guilty when these anxieties hit. Keep in mind that it is normal for babies to go through this. Usually they stop crying within 10 minutes.

MATT, AGE 19

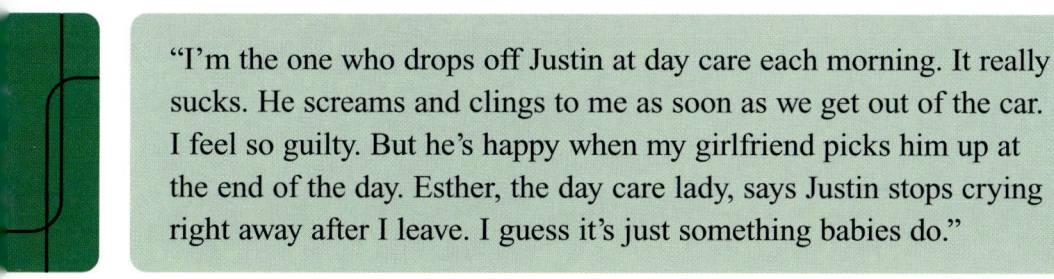

"I'm the one who drops off Justin at day care each morning. It really sucks. He screams and clings to me as soon as we get out of the car. I feel so guilty. But he's happy when my girlfriend picks him up at the end of the day. Esther, the day care lady, says Justin stops crying right away after I leave. I guess it's just something babies do."

Fun and Games

Reading to your baby can help his language development. Choose books with familiar objects. Don't choose books with too many pictures on one page. Let your baby hold the books. Choose board books, cloth books, or vinyl books. These he can safely put in his mouth.

Behavior Changes and Positive Discipline

When babies at this stage cry, it is best to respond quickly. They usually have needs that are not being met. Some people may think responding quickly spoils your baby. That is not true. Your baby needs to know you are there for her.

Your baby wants to touch everything she sees at this stage. Allow her to explore. Do not, however, allow her to damage property or put herself at risk. Therefore, you need to teach her. It is best to distract her if she is moving toward something undesirable. Use other toys or activities for distraction.

Try rarely to say no. If you say it too often, it will lose its meaning. You may need to remove things that are always a temptation. You can move them back when your baby is older.

Try to reserve serious discipline for times when your baby could be in danger. For example, your baby obviously shouldn't touch electrical outlets. Say no firmly and remove her from the situation. She will not learn from one or two episodes. You need to repeat these steps over and over before she learns. Make sure your baby hears no every time she goes to the undesirable activity. Be consistent and quick with your response.

It also is important to reward positive behavior. Hug your baby and thank her for hesitating before touching an outlet. Praise her and thank her for being gentle with a pet. Her desire to please you soon will drive much of her behavior.

Points to Consider

Why should you use safety gates near stairways at this stage? What are some other ways to make your home safer for your baby?

What are some ways to play with your baby during this stage?

Why should you limit the number of times you say no to your baby? What are some ways you can reward positive behavior?

NOTE

At publication, all resources listed here were accurate and appropriate to the topics covered in this book. Addresses and phone numbers may change. When visiting Internet sites and links, use good judgment.

INTERNET SITES

Baby Place
www.baby-place.com
Provides information on pregnancy, birth, and babies

BabyZone!
www.babyzone.com
Contains family planning, pregnancy, and parenting information

Parent Soup
www.parentsoup.com
Offers advice, message boards, and chat for parents and expecting parents

Useful Addresses

American Academy of Pediatrics National Headquarters
141 Northwest Point Boulevard
Elk Grove Village, IL 60007
www.aap.org

Canadian Institute of Child Health
885 Meadowlands Drive
Suite 512
Ottawa, ON K2C 3N2
CANADA
www.cich.ca

La Leche League International
1400 North Meacham Road
Schaumburg, IL 60173-4048
www.lalecheleague.org

National Child Care Information Center
243 Church Street Northwest
2nd Floor
Vienna, VA 22180
1-800-616-2242
www.nccic.org

The Nemours Foundation Center for Children's Health Media
Alfred I. duPont Hospital for Children
1600 Rockland Road
Wilmington, DE 19803
www.kidshealth.org

Zero to Three: National Center for Infants, Toddlers, and Families
734 15th Street Northwest
Washington, DC 20005
www.zerotothree.org

For Further Reading

Endersbe, Julie. *Teen Fathers: Getting Involved.* Mankato, MN: Capstone, 2000.

Endersbe, Julie. *Teen Mothers: Raising a Baby.* Mankato, MN: Capstone, 2000.

Fairview Health Services. *Caring for You and Your Baby: From Pregnancy Through the First Year of Life.* Minneapolis: Fairview Press, 1997.

Lindsay, Jeanne Warren. *Your Baby's First Year: A Guide for Teenage Parents.* Buena Park, CA: Morning Glory Press, 1998.

Thoennes Keller, Kristin. *Health Care for Infants and Toddlers.* Mankato, MN: Capstone, 2001.

GLOSSARY

anxiety (ang-ZYE-uh-tee)—a feeling of worry or fear

babble (BAB-uhl)—the gibberish sounds a baby makes

baby-proofing (BAY-bee PROOF-ing)—making an area safe for a baby to be in

circumcision (sur-kuhm-SI-zhuhn)—the process of surgically removing the foreskin from a penis

colostrum (kuh-LOSS-truhm)—the thin, yellow fluid that breasts produce before breast milk comes in

foreskin (FOR-skin)—the skin on the tip of the penis

formula (FOR-myuh-luh)—a liquid substitute for mother's milk

genitals (JEN-i-tuhlz)—the sex organs located on the outside of the body

immunization (im-yuh-nuh-ZAY-shuhn)—a shot given to people to help prevent a certain disease

infant (IN-fuhnt)—a newborn child; babies are considered infants until they can walk.

mobile (MOH-beel)—a toy for babies to look at but not touch; mobiles are made of several items at different heights that hang from a central wire or thread.

solid (SOL-id)—a nutritional, nonliquid food that a baby eats

Sudden Infant Death Syndrome (SIDS) (SUHD-uhn IN-fuhnt DETH SIN-drohm [SIDZ])—a condition in which babies die with no explanation; usually SIDS happens when babies are sleeping.

teething (TEETH-ing)—the time when a baby's new teeth come in

umbilical cord (uhm-BIL-uh-kuhl KORD)—the tube that connects an unborn baby to its mother's body; what's left of the cord after birth must be cleaned until it falls off.

INDEX

attachment, 5, 13, 21, 24, 40, 47

babbling, 41, 46, 51, 55
babies
    newborn, 5–11, 13–19, 21–22, 25
    1 to 3 months, 39–43
    4 to 7 months, 16, 26, 34, 36, 45–51
    8 to 12 months, 16, 34, 35, 36, 53–59
baby-proofing, 17–18
bathing, 9–10
behavior changes
    4 to 7 months, 50–51
    8 to 12 months, 58–59
bottlefeeding, 8, 16, 23, 24–25, 26, 33, 36
    and burping, 26–27, 28
    how much to feed, 25
    at night, 7, 25, 42, 49, 50
bowel movements, 8, 32
breastfeeding, 8, 16, 21–24, 26, 33, 36
    and burping, 23, 26–27
    how much to feed, 22–23
    at night, 7, 42, 49
    and supplemental bottles, 23
breast milk
    expressing, 21, 23
    storing and thawing, 23–24
burping, 23, 26–27, 28

calming your child, 6–7, 48–49
car seats, 18
child abuse and neglect, 17. *See also* shaking; spanking
choking, 16, 18, 25, 29, 34, 46
colic, 6. *See also* crying
crawling, 45, 53
cribs, 7, 18, 42, 48

crying, 6–7, 17, 23, 42, 57, 58
    kinds of, 6
    at nighttime, 48–49
    and separation anxiety, 47, 56, 57

day care, 18–19, 57
diapers and diaper rash, 8, 9, 11, 46
discipline, positive
    4 to 7 months, 50–51
    8 to 12 months, 58–59
doctors, 5, 6, 14, 15, 16, 26, 31, 49, 51

ear infections, 25, 29
electrocution/electric outlets, 17, 58, 59

feeding your child
    and burping, 26–27, 28
    to comfort them, 6, 7
    how much, 13, 22–23, 25, 34
    at night, 7, 25, 42, 49, 50
    solids, 26, 31–36
    water and juice, 26
    when your child is sick, 16
    See also bottlefeeding; breastfeeding; hiccuping; spitting up
fevers, 15–16
fingers, using, 32, 34, 45, 53, 55
food sensitivity, 32
formula. *See* bottlefeeding
fruits, 31, 32, 33, 35, 36

gates, 18, 53
genitals, 11, 46

health, 13–16
hiccuping, 26, 27
holding your child, 5, 6–7, 42
    other people, 6, 13, 19

INDEX

immunizations, 14

lactation consultants, 22, 24
language development
    1 to 3 months, 41
    4 to 7 months, 46
    8 to 12 months, 55–56
    See also reading

medication, 15, 49
microwaving formula, 24, 25
muscle development, 39, 45, 53

nail care, 10
naps, 48

personality, 47
physical changes
    1 to 3 months, 39
    4 to 7 months, 45–46
    8 to 12 months, 53
playing, 40, 42, 47, 55, 56
poison, 17, 18

reading, 40, 58
rectal thermometer, 14–15
rice cereal, 31, 36

safety, 9–10, 16–19, 42, 53
saying no, 17, 50–51, 58
seeing and hearing
    1 to 3 months, 40
    4 to 7 months, 46
shaking, 7, 17
sickness
    fevers and, 15–16, 49
    preventing, 13
    and taking temperature, 14–15
sitting, 45, 46, 53

sleeping
    1 to 3 months, 7, 16, 42–43
    4 to 7 months, 7, 16, 48–49
    position of newborns while, 7, 16
smoking, 14, 18, 40
social and emotional development
    1 to 3 months, 42
    4 to 7 months, 47
    8 to 12 months, 56–57
solids, 31–36
    how much and how often, 34
    starting, 31–33
spanking, 51
spitting up, 15, 26, 28
spoiling your child, 5, 58
stairs, 53
strangulation, 16, 18, 46
stress, 5, 13, 34
Sudden Infant Death Syndrome
    (SIDS), 16
suffocation, 7, 42

talking with your child, 5, 40, 41, 42, 46, 55
teething, 49–50
temperature, 14–15
tooth decay, 25, 26, 50
toys, 7, 42, 45, 47, 53, 55, 56–57, 58
traveling, 18
trust, 5, 6, 42

umbilical cord, 9–10
urination, 8, 11

vegetables, 32, 35, 36

walking, 54, 55
words, first, 55, 56